Black Death

by

Martyn Beardsley

Illustrated by Martin Remphry

First published in 2010 in Great Britain by
Barrington Stoke Ltd
18 Walker Street, Edinburgh, EH3 7LP

www.barringtonstoke.co.uk

ISBN: 978-1-84299-765-9

Printed in Great Britain by Bell & Bain Ltd

Contents

Chapter 1
Arrival
June 1348

The little ship arrived at the port of Melcombe Regis, Dorset, in lashing, bone-chilling rain. While sailors took in the sails, young Will Burstock was up on deck getting the ship ready to dock after its voyage to France.

Once his work was done and the older men wandered away to the drinking taverns or their homes, Will hung around the

harbour. He was wet, cold and miserable –
yet in no hurry to go home. "Home" didn't
mean the same thing to Will any more.

His mother had died of a fever three years ago, when he was just twelve. Then, last year, his father had made one of his regular voyages to France selling wool. Will had been joining him on these trips just lately, but this time he stayed at home to look after his younger sister Anne. Will's father never came back.

For many months there had been tales of a strange sickness spreading through Europe. Will's father and three other members of the crew had fallen victim to the frightening new disease, and their ship had returned without them.

Will and Anne were left alone, unable to pay the rent on their little family home. They were sent to live three miles away with their mother's brother in the tiny village of Winterton. Will had seen little of Uncle Thomas and Aunt Jenny before. Will's father and Uncle Thomas and Aunt Jenny had never got on with each other, and it seemed "the Old Miseries" as they were known, were no more keen on Will and Anne. They already had three children of their own so Will and Anne meant more mouths to feed and less space in the house. Uncle Thomas and Aunt Jenny ignored them most of the time, and Will noticed that he and Anne always seemed to get the leftover food – and not as much of it as everyone else. He often went to bed still feeling hungry.

So, despite being keen to see Anne again, Will didn't head straight back to Winterton. Spotting his friend Robert sheltering from the rain in a doorway, Will slung his kit bag onto his back and went over to join him.

"I bet old Edmund had you working hard as ever," said Robert.

Edmund Blackworth was the owner of the ship. He was known for being strict and grumpy. But he had known Will's father well, and Will had noticed how much kinder the captain had been towards him on this voyage.

"He's all right."

As they were saying this, Edmund Blackworth himself came down the gang-plank from the ship. Just then, a large black rat came scuttling down from the ship, quickly followed by another, and then another.

Will grinned and tapped Robert on the shoulder. "Look!"

The first rat scampered between Blackworth's legs. He turned to see what was happening, and as the other rats ran towards him the captain was startled and almost lost his balance. He began wobbling and swaying, with legs and arms waving in all directions. Just when it seemed he was going to topple into the water, he managed to regain his balance.

"Shame!" chuckled Robert. "Would have been fun to see him go for a swim!"

The rats darted among the crates and barrels on the harbour, vanishing from sight.

"Filthy, flea-ridden things," said Will. "They were all over the ship as always."

"Rats are clever little animals, you know," said Robert. "I'm sure they don't really do any harm ..."

Will stayed the night with Robert on his father's farm. The next morning he went back into Melcombe to collect his pay for the voyage from Edmund Blackworth. As he was walking past the White Hart Inn, a young maid came running out. Seeing Will she stopped, gripping his sleeve. "Have you seen Stephen the Apothecary?" she cried. There was panic in her voice.

"No. Who is ill?"

"It's Mistress Helen, the inn-keeper's wife. She needs medicine. They say it is the Black Death, come from France!"

Will felt a cold shiver pass through his body as if he had been hit by a sudden icy wind. The same sickness which had taken his father. The Black Death, which seemed so frightening yet so far away. Was it now right here in Melcombe?

Chapter 2
God's Anger

Winterton was a tiny village on the road to Dorchester. Most of the people who lived there made a living either by farming or going to sea. Uncle Thomas was different – he worked as a candle-maker. He made good money – although you'd never know it. He was well known in the village for being mean.

As Will avoided the puddles along the road towards Winterton, he spotted his eleven-year-old sister Anne in the distance, feeding the chickens and pigs in the yard at the back of the cottage. She must have noticed her brother at the same time, because she dumped the bag of feed and raced across the field towards him, her face beaming with delight.

"*Will!*"

They hugged each other tightly, and Will lifted Anne off her feet and swung her round and round. He was met with a different greeting when he entered the cottage. Aunt Jenny was sewing in a plain wooden chair by the window, trying to make the most of the gloomy daylight. Uncle Thomas only allowed the lighting of candles when it was completely dark. She looked up only briefly.

"Oh, it's you. I expected you sooner."

Uncle Thomas treated Will and Anne as if they were not wanted – but Aunt Jenny seemed to *really* hate them.

"I stayed in Melcombe to get my wages, Aunt."

She put her work down and held out her hand.

They always took most of the money he made – to cover the cost of his food and so on, they said. Will knew they took far more of his pay than they needed, but he dare not say anything in case they kicked him and Anne out.

Aunt Jenny stared up at him with narrowed eyes. "This is all?"

For a second, Will thought of lying, but he knew it was wrong. "I bought food and drink in Melcombe, and a small gift for Anne in France."

"Hmm. No gift for your uncle or me, I suppose?"

Will didn't reply, but stared at her defiantly. That was answer enough.

"It will all come out of your share of the money. It's only fair."

There's nothing fair about my share of the money, Will thought.

"I know, Aunt," he said.

A couple of weeks later, Will took Anne to the harbour. She loved seeing the ships, and

Edmund Blackworth had promised Will that she could go on the *Joseph and Mary*.

"Can I climb to the top of the mast?" she asked as they walked down the hill towards the town. She was skipping along, playing with the cup and ball he had brought her back from France.

"I'm not sure what Captain Blackworth would say about that," smiled Will.

Anne continued to chatter about going aboard the ship – but Will was no longer listening. They had arrived in Melcombe and he suddenly felt worried, though he couldn't say exactly why. It was just a feeling that something wasn't right. The White Hart's door was closed, which it never was during the day. And instead of the normal comings and goings, people were standing in huddles, grim-faced and talking in low voices – the way people did when something important has happened.

Robert came running up. His face was pale, his eyes wide.

"It *is* the Black Death!" He glanced back, almost as if the deadly disease was chasing him. Will had never seen Robert look so afraid.

"How do you know?"

"Mistress Helen at the White Hart has died, and her husband is near to death. Three other people are already going the same way.

They have a terrible fever and headache, then boils like onions appear under their armpits. The swellings become hot, red and painful. Next they turn almost black and burst, and then – "

"All right, all right, I believe you." Will didn't want to hear any more. It was frightening Anne as well as himself. It would be bad enough at any time, but this was how their father had died …

"Will *we* catch it?" Anne gasped. "What shall we do?"

"Some say it is God's anger," Robert told them. "People have turned away from His teachings and become selfish and dishonest."

Will was suddenly glad he had not lied to Aunt Jenny about his pay. Might that save him from the Black Death?

"But others say it lives in the foul air which is in the ships and breathed in by the crews ..." Robert darted Will a fearful look, as if only just realising what his words meant "... who have returned from France." Without warning, Robert turned and ran away.

Will's heart sank. How could his own best friend be afraid of him?

A group of men were gathered near the *Joseph and Mary*, deep in talk. Robert's pounding footsteps made some look round, and then Will saw one of them staring right at him. The man worked in the harbour and knew that Will sailed on the *Joseph and Mary*. The staring man said something to the group, and they all turned their gaze on Will now, too. He couldn't hear what they were saying, but something in their eyes stabbed at his heart like an eagle's claw. He quickly took Anne by the arm and lead her back towards Winterton.

Chapter 3
Cast Out

It was dinner time and Will was shifting uneasily in his seat. It was a hard wooden chair – the only sort that Uncle Thomas would have in the house. But that wasn't why Will was worried. He and Anne kept exchanging sly glances. What would happen when their aunt and uncle found out about the Black Death?

Would most people blame God for bringing it to England? Or would they blame those – like Will – who had just returned from France? What sort of gossip would reach the ears of Thomas and Jenny?

As he ate, he realised that the knife was shaking in his hand.

The Black Death came to Winterton the following month. First a young farm worker fell ill, then the old widow who lived next to the church. When a servant in the large manor house outside the village became sick, she was quickly sent home. The Lord and his family shut up the great house and left – no one knew where to.

Will and Anne returned from collecting wood for the fire one morning. Will knew something was wrong when he saw Uncle Thomas and Aunt Jenny waiting for him outside the cottage. They had a small pile of items at their feet.

"Those are our things!" Anne cried. "What are they doing? It's our clothes and my toys – everything!"

"I don't know," Will replied – but he had a pretty good idea.

When he was about ten metres away, Uncle Thomas shouted for him to stop. "Do not come any closer to us. Take your things and leave Winterton immediately."

"*Plague bringer!*" Aunt Jenny hissed.

Will started to approach him. "But Uncle, I – "

"*Do NOT* come any nearer – breathing your foul, deadly air on us!"

By now, other villagers were beginning to gather round – but not too close. Anne looked round at the growing crowd and began to whimper. Will gave her hand a squeeze.

"I haven't brought the Black Death!" he protested. But he wasn't even sure himself and knew it sounded half-hearted, almost like a lie.

Just then the church bell tolled. They were burying Henry Langley the farm worker – and his mother and brother.

"You had better be gone before this day is done, or we'll drive you out," growled a voice. Will turned and recognised Matthew Black, the miller. Will often visited his windmill to get flour for baking bread. He had always been cheerful and friendly, asking Will for tales of his trips across the sea. Now, his face was dark with anger.

"We have nowhere to go!" Anne shivered.

"*Go back to France, then!*" Aunt Jenny screeched, and there were nods of agreement.

If Will didn't take Anne away quickly, there was no knowing what might happen. "Come, Anne," he said as calmly as his shaky voice would allow.

He slowly walked towards the little bundle of clothes and other things from the cottage, lying on the wet ground. It was everything he and Anne owned in the world. As soon as he did so, Uncle Thomas and Aunt Jenny backed away.

He and Anne gathered everything up and began to walk away. There were only two directions out of Winterton: the road to the north, which Will had never taken and didn't know what lay along it; and the road to the south – Melcombe and the coast. Clutching Anne's little hand, cold with fear, this was the road he took.

They didn't look back, but Will's neck stiffened at the thought of all those angry eyes watching them.

It was Anne who spoke first. "It will be all right. We shall be happier away from Aunt Jenny and Uncle Thomas anyway."

Will was surprised to hear her quiet, brave voice saying such words. Yet despite her attempt at sounding cheerful, he saw tears in her eyes.

"Yes. I know lots of people around the harbour. Something will turn up …"

As he spoke, he heard the church bells toll, marking another burial. But it wasn't the Winterton church. It was coming from down the hill in Melcombe Regis.

Chapter 4
On the Run

Will led Anne across the fields towards the little farm where his friend Robert lived.

The idea had come to him just before they reached Melcombe. If anyone would look after them, at least for a while, it was Robert. Despite the fact that Robert seemed afraid Will had brought the Black Death back from France with him, he knew the family and felt sure they would be much more understanding than Uncle Thomas, Aunt Jenny and the people of Winterton. But now

Will had something else to worry about. He had begun to get a strange feeling in his right armpit. The thought of what it might mean was too terrifying even to think about – yet he couldn't help looking at Anne and wondering. If he had the Black Death, had he passed it on to his little sister by now too? For now, he pushed such thoughts out of his mind.

But there was no one about on the farm. Normally there would be many workers on the land at this time of the year, yet now it was deserted. There were weeds as tall as the crops, and hopping, squabbling black crows had the fields to themselves. Will led Anne carefully towards the farmhouse, where he caught sight of Robert's dog. It was painfully thin, whining and scratching pitifully at the door.

Will knocked, but it somehow felt as pointless as shouting into an empty room. He turned the knob and found the door unlocked.

"Wait here," he told Anne quietly. He had a very bad feeling about this ...

Anne waited at the door hugging her trembling, skinny body, while Will crept inside. The house was dark and silent, and an unpleasant smell hung in the air.

Will saw the first body sprawled at the end of the landing upstairs.

He didn't go near it, but he knew from the shape and the clothes that it was Robert's father. He peered round the door of the main bedroom. A hasty glance revealed the outline of a second body on the big four-poster bed, covered by a blanket. Turning sharply away, Will found himself facing Robert's bedroom, which he had been in many times. He put his hand to the doorknob ... then pulled it back again. He somehow knew that Robert was lying in there like the others, and he couldn't bear to see him like that. He walked back downstairs on wobbly legs.

"We must go."

"Why? What's happened? Have they gone away to escape the Black Death?"

Will was gazing about the farmyard where he and Robert used to play, his eyes stinging and a tightness forming in his throat. "Yes," he said. "They've gone away."

Melcombe was like a town after a war has swept through it. Few people were about; bundles of wool lay piled on the dock, sagging and wet through from the rain; a deserted ship in the harbour swung at anchor, her sails flapping loosely, half her goods still to be loaded. Had her crew all died, Will wondered, or simply fled on hearing that the Black Death had reached Melcombe?

As Will and Anne wandered through the streets, they almost bumped into Stephen the Apothecary coming out of Widow Rudd's house.

"Stephen!" cried Anne. "Stephen will have some medicines to help people!"

But on overhearing this Stephen shook his head sadly. "Betty Rudd has had a fever, and now a swelling – a bubo – has appeared on her neck. I have cut the bubo to let some of the sickness drain away, and washed her with vinegar and water – but in truth, nothing seems to work in the end. Melcombe is not a safe place for you, Will …"

"Perhaps if we stay away from everyone we won't catch it."

"Perhaps – but that is not what I meant. People are holding the crew of the *Joseph and Mary* to blame, and they are angry. The crew who haven't fallen to the Black Death have fled or been chased out."

"Even Captain Blackworth?"

"Edmund Blackworth is dead."

Will couldn't help scratching under his arm, and Stephen noticed this.

"Let me see, Will."

He saw Anne's eyes widen with horror, and shuddered. "No ... It's nothing."

But Stephen made him open his shirt so that he could look. And he was glad he did.

"It is just a rash, that's all," the apothecary smiled. "Nothing to worry about!"

Will's spirits rose, and he suddenly felt as if he was walking on air.

Stephen went on his way, and Will and Anne carried on theirs – though Will had no idea what that "way" was. The streets which he had known all his life no longer seemed familiar to him. The world itself felt like a different place and he was an outsider in it. The only time he had ever seen the town so deserted was on a Sunday when everyone was in church. Today wasn't a Sunday, but the church bells were ringing – for the dead. Yet Will felt drawn in that direction. At least the church was a place of peace, and the priest a man of wisdom and kindness.

As they rounded a corner and the church came into view, Will saw a group of people across the street, shuffling slowly in the same direction. They were following a coffin which was being carried on the shoulders of six men. Most of the group had their heads bowed down, eyes gazing at the muddy street beneath their feet. A woman happened to look up and catch Will's eye. It was someone he knew by sight though he had never spoken to her and didn't know her name. But the look in her eye sent a shiver through his body.

"*There's one of them!*" she shrieked.

The whole funeral party looked towards Will and Anne now, and a low murmur rose amongst them which sounded like the buzz of bees when a hive has been disturbed.

Anne clutched Will's arm. *"I'm frightened ..."*

Three men began to move away from the main group. Another woman tried to hold the biggest of them back, but he shook his arm free and led the others towards Will and Anne, his face as dark as thunder.

Will and Anne were coming to a dark, narrow lane which he knew led round the back of the Customs House. *"Get ready to run,"* he whispered. He forced himself to walk at his normal pace the last few steps to the lane, with the three men advancing on them with menace in their eyes. Then, as soon as they were level with the side-street, Will cried, *"Now!"* and yanked Anne after him as they set off at a sprint. He clutched her hand tightly. She couldn't run nearly as fast as him and staying with her might mean that they both got caught – but better that than leave her to them while he fled alone.

The footsteps behind them pounded closer. Once or twice Will tried to make Anne go too fast and she stumbled, and Will had to ease off a little. If she fell, the men behind were closing on them so quickly that it would be the end.

What would they do if they *did* catch them? Will didn't like to think about it, and put all his efforts into staying ahead of them.

When they got to the end of the lane he steered sharply to the right, where he knew that across the street there was yet another narrow path between two rows of houses. Will tugged Anne into one of the gardens. He had thought of knocking on the door and begging for protection – but what if the people inside were as angry with him as those men who were chasing?

He could now see that there was a narrow gap between the two cottages. Will and Anne dashed into this – there was even a chance that the chasing group might not have come round the corner in time to see where they had gone. Will prayed that this was so, because by now he could feel Anne getting slower and hear her struggling for breath. She couldn't go on like this much longer.

Will dared to pause for a second once they were beyond the cottages and out into another street. He glanced back down the space between the two buildings – just in time to see the men running on past.

The danger was over for the present and he and Anne were able to walk and recover their breath. But they had to keep moving. The men were soon bound to realise they had taken a wrong turn. And anyway, how many more people like that were they going to meet in Melcombe? How many more people blamed Will and his crew for bring the Black Death to England? And were they right?

Chapter 5
The Farm

The landscape became less and less familiar the further Will and Anne walked with their backs to the town where they had been born.

Along country lanes, across muddy fields, beside rivers he and Anne trudged. Their legs became heavy and their empty bellies gurgled in complaint. At first, Will had simply been relieved to get away from danger. But the further they wandered from the places they knew, like ships drifting away from sight of land, the heavier his heart became. They had no money, nowhere to sleep, no one to turn to. For two days Will avoided villages and farms for fear that the Black Death had reached them and he might get the blame. They drank water from streams and ate fruit and raw vegetables they found at the edges of farmers' fields. It was stealing in a way, but Will felt less guilty than he might have done because it was clear that none of the farmland was being looked after. The crops would end up rotting in the ground.

In the end, living on scraps was not enough. Anne never complained, patiently following Will in whichever direction he decided they should go. But he had noticed how pale she was, how dark around the eyes, and how slow and uncertain her step had become. He felt little stronger himself, and he knew they could not go on like this. But as hard as their journey had been, the truth was that they probably had not travelled many miles from Melcombe. Most places around here, he felt sure, would be very wary of strangers. So Will came up with a plan.

It would only work for a few days, but at least it would give him time to think. The next farm they came to, they would hide out in some old shed or hut, and steal whatever food they could at night or whenever no one was about. At least that way they could build up their strength before moving on.

And it wasn't long before they came across a lonely little farmhouse by a stream which had an old barn a little way away. They waited in some nearby woods till darkness came, then crept into the rundown building and made a bed for themselves in the hay. That night Will had his best sleep in a long time.

In the morning they kept watch on the farmhouse. The farmer came out first. He was a short old man with snow-white hair sticking out beneath his hat. He walked off into the fields, and about half an hour later a woman came out of the house carrying a basket with scraps of food in it. She must be the farmer's wife, and she went round to the farmyard on the other side of the house and began throwing the food to the hens and other animals there. Will made his move.

He dashed out as quickly yet silently as he could, slipped into the farmhouse, and was

back with Anne within a minute carrying half
a loaf of bread and two strips of bacon. The
bread was hard and nearly stale and the
bacon was greasy – but at that moment it
was the tastiest meal Will had ever had.

This went on for five days.

"How come they don't realise some food is missing?" Anne asked Will eventually.

"Perhaps they do. But they'll only know where it's going to if we get caught!"

"It's not fair though, taking so much food from that little old man and woman. I think we should find somewhere else, Will."

He nodded. He had been putting this moment off because he felt so safe here. But it was stealing after all. They had to find a place where no one had heard of the Black Death – or the boy who had brought it to England – and find work. He decided he would make one last trip into the farmhouse to get them some food for their journey.

But this time it was different.

He tip-toed into the kitchen and saw some sliced meat on a large plate, together with the usual loaf of bread. But just as he was reaching for it, he heard something which made him stop as still as a statue.

"*You only had to ask.*"

Will spun round and found himself face-to-face with the farmer, standing in a doorway leading from another room. Will was about to scramble out as fast as he could when something made him change his mind.

The little old man's blue eyes twinkled like stars on a summer's night, and there was even the hint of a smile on his face. This man wasn't going to chase him like the others.

"B–but ..."

"I may be getting old and slow-witted, lad, but I knew *someone* was taking my grub! Today, I decided to go out the front door and straight back in by the back and find out who it was. I suppose you're running away from the Black Death? You wouldn't be the first."

By now the farmer's wife had also come into the kitchen. She seemed to be in on her husband's plan. Will told them most of the story, but couldn't bring himself to speak about the worst part – that he himself might to blame for everything that had happened. Even so, as he told his tale he felt tears welling up in his eyes – tears he had been fighting to hide from Anne for many days.

"*We have nowhere to go …*" he said, his words turning into sobs and splutters. He found himself being folded into the arms and bosom of the farmer's wife. It was so nice not to have to be strong any more. He felt like a child again, and the woman's hug reminded him of being in his mother's arms.

And this was how Will and Anne found themselves living on Joseph Smith's farm. For two years Will helped the old man in the fields and Anne helped Mrs Smith around the house and in the yard. They were firm but very kind, and glad of the help. It was almost like having a mother and father again. Will even finally admitted his fears about being one of those who was spreading the terrible new disease.

"I reckon I'd have caught it by now if you were the plague-bringer," smiled Farmer Smith. "Anyway, even if it were true, it's not like you did it on purpose. Some people might blame you, but I'm sure God wouldn't."

The Black Death swept the country like a forest fire, not caring whether people thought if it was sent by God to punish them or if it was some kind of disease in the air. Farmer Smith normally took the food he grew to market, but now he kept everything to feed the four of them and his animals. They kept themselves to themselves, and the plague left them alone.

And then one day, Joseph Smith decided it was time for Will to find out what had happened to Aunt Jenny and Uncle Thomas. Will didn't want to because of the way they had treated him. But the farmer said they were his only relatives and it was the right thing to do, and Will knew he was correct.

Because they didn't know what they would find, Anne stayed behind with Mrs Smith.

When the pair of them reached Melcombe, Will thought for a moment they had taken a wrong turn somewhere and reached a different town. There was grass growing in the streets. Houses were boarded up, some had holes in their roofs. There was a half-sunken ship rotting in the harbour. Worse still, there were bodies lying by the doors of some of the houses. It seemed that there weren't even enough people left to bury the dead.

This was not the place he had left behind. But the town still had some life in it. A small ship flying a French flag was unloading. There were only half the usual number of men around to help with the work, but it was a good sign. And there was a group of people following the priest through the streets – all bare-footed and with eyes cast down, praying

loudly to God for forgiveness for their sins and begging for an end to the suffering.

As they made their way to Winterton Will passed several people who knew him, but there were no more accusing looks or shouts. It was as if there was no longer any energy left to waste on anger – it was all people could do to stay alive, and they were all in it together.

His aunt and uncle and their children were no longer alive, as Will somehow had known. The door of their once neat little cottage was hanging off at a crazy angle, just held up by one rusty hinge. There was hardly anyone about, and the village was over-grown with weeds. Starved sheep and cows, having escaped from their fields in search of food, lay dead in the main street. But smoke rose from a couple of chimneys, and from somewhere not too far away they could hear the sound of wood being chopped.

"It's been a terrible old time," Farmer Smith commented as he gazed at the sad scenes around them. "But people will bounce back. It will take time, but they always do in the end."

They returned to the farm, and Joseph Smith continued to be like a father to Will and Anne. And like a father to a son, Mr Smith left him his farm when he died. So it was that when the food markets started up again Farmer Will Burstock was one of the first to arrive, and his vegetables were said to be the finest for miles around.

Black Death Facts

The Black Death is often said to have been caused by rats. In fact, it was *caused* by disease-carrying fleas – but *spread* by the rats the fleas lived on.

The Black Death is thought to have started in Mongolia. It then spread to China which is close by, and from there across large parts of the world.

There is a story which may well be true that the Black Death was brought to Britain by rats on a ship from France, which arrived at Melcombe Regis near Weymouth in Dorset, on the 25th June 1348.

When the rats died, the blood-sucking insects looked for a new place to live – including the warm, juicy bodies of humans!

People did not know what caused the Black Death because they did not understand the causes of most illnesses in those days. It would be hundreds of years before scientists worked out what caused diseases and how to prevent or cure them.

Some people believed that whipping themselves to show God how sorry they were for their sins might cure the Black Death. Others believed that being cut and letting some of the "bad" blood out might work (for a long time being bled was thought to help cure almost *every* illness).

And if that didn't work you could try putting a hen next to the swelling to draw the badness out, then just to be on the safe side also drink your own wee twice a day until cured!

Victims who found very painful red swellings in their groins, armpits or neck knew they only had days left to live. (But a few lucky people did recover.) The swellings turned purple or black and then burst, with disgusting smelly goo leaking out. Victims quickly became sicker, until, within a week, they died.

No one can be sure how many people in Britain died, but it may have been a third or even nearly half of the population. About six million people lived in England then, so two to three million must have died. Look around your classroom and imagine half of them suddenly gone forever, like Will's best friend!

The Black Death lasted for two years in Britain. It did strike again, but never in such a deadly way as on that first frightening occasion.

AUTHOR FACT FILE
MARTYN BEARDSLEY

What is the worst illness you've ever had?

I've been very lucky and never had anything worse than the flu. I try to eat well and exercise – so maybe it works!

Which of the doctors' cures for the Black Death would you have least liked to try?

Drinking my own wee doesn't sound quite as good as a nice cup of tea.

Which time in history would you most like to visit?

I once had a dream that I was living in an Anglo-Saxon village. The dream felt so real, I'd love to go back and check out how close it was to the truth.

If you went to sea, who would be your ideal cabin-mate?

A Victorian explorer and sailor called Sir John Franklin. I've written a book about him. Not only is he a hero of mine, he'd also know how to steer the ship, so that would be handy!

ILLUSTRATOR FACT FILE
MARTIN REMPHRY

What is the worst illness you've ever had?

I have been quite lucky with my health, but as a boy I did have asthma. Sometimes it was very difficult to breathe and it felt as if my chest was getting tighter and tighter.

Which of the doctors' cures for the Black Death would you have least liked to try?

Holding a chicken onto your boils must have been bad enough, but cutting open a vein must have been very painful.

Which time in history would you most like to visit?

The Dark Ages. They are called 'Dark' because we know very little about them. Perhaps I might get a chance to meet the real King Arthur.

If you went to sea, who would be your ideal cabin-mate?

An expert sailor. I am no good at sailing!

Barrington Stoke would like to thank all its readers for commenting on the manuscript before publication and in particular:

Adam Blower

Steven Brookes

Josh Butler

Connor Campbell

Rebecca Collingwood

Bethany Dalgliesh

Kyle Dawson

Poppy Lou Feather

Damien Floyde

Sue Ford

Luke Harper

Raimonds Ivbulis

George Lindsay

Jenny Linsley

Joseph Mills

Neil Musk

Damien Newman

Kyle Parson

Liberty Gerrard-Pickering

Issy Sleightholme

Beth Southern

Chloe Vincent

Jessica Yeomans

Become a Consultant!

Would you like to be a consultant? Ask your parent, carer or teacher to contact us at the email address below – we'd love to hear from them! They can also find out more by visiting our website.

schools@barringtonstoke.co.uk
www.barringtonstoke.co.uk